BEARCUB BIOS

U.S. REPRESENTATIVE

by Rachel Rose

Consultant: Beth Gambro
Reading Specialist, Yorkville, Illinois

Minneapolis, Minnesota

Teaching Tips

BEFORE READING

- Discuss what a biography is. What kinds of things might a biography tell a reader?
- Look through the glossary together. Read and discuss the words.
- Go on a picture walk, looking through the pictures to discuss vocabulary and make predictions about the text.

DURING READING

- Encourage readers to point to each word as it is read. Stop occasionally to ask readers to point to a specific word in the text.
- If a reader encounters an unknown word, ask them to look at the rest of the page. Are there any clues to help them understand?

AFTER READING

- Check for understanding.
  - Where was Alexandria Ocasio-Cortez born?
  - What does she do?
  - What does she care about?
- Ask the readers to think deeper.
  - If you met Alexandria, what question would you like to ask her? Why?

Credits:
Cover and title page, © SOPA Images Limited/Alamy Stock Photo and © Noiel/Shutterstock; 3, © lev radin/Shutterstock; 5, © DON EMMERT/Getty Images; 7, © Rainmaker Photo/MediaPunch/AP Images; 9, © Samantha Burkardt/Getty Images; 10–11, © DenisTangneyJr/iStock; 12, © DON EMMERT/Getty Images; 15, © Zach Gibson/Getty Images; 16–17, © Win McNamee/Getty Images; 19, © Rachael Warriner/Shutterstock; 21, © NBC NewsWire/Getty Images ; 22, © SAUL LOEB/Getty Images; 23TL, © ANDRZEJ WOJCICKI/Getty Images; 23TM, © BenGoode/iStock; 23TR, © uschools/iStock; 23BL, © adamkaz/iStock; and 23BR, © FatCamera/iStock.

Library of Congress Cataloging-in-Publication Data

Names: Rose, Rachel, 1968– author. Title: Alexandria Ocasio-Cortez : U.S. Representative / by Rachel Rose. Description: Bearcub books. | Minneapolis, Minnesota : Bearport Publishing Company, 2021. | Series: Bearcub bios | Includes bibliographical references and index. Identifiers: LCCN 2019057649 (print) | LCCN 2019057650 (ebook) | ISBN 9781642809763 (library binding) | ISBN 9781642809879 (paperback) | ISBN 9781642809985 (ebook) Subjects: LCSH: Ocasio-Cortez, Alexandria, 1989—-Juvenile literature. | Women legislators—United States—Biography—Juvenile literature. | Legislators—United States—Biography—Juvenile literature. | United States. Congress. House—Biography—Juvenile literature. Classification: LCC E901.1.O27 R67 2021 (print) | LCC E901.1.O27 (ebook) | DDC 328.73/092 [B]—dc23 LC record available at https://lccn.loc.gov/2019057649LC ebook record available at https://lccn.loc.gov/2019057650

Copyright © 2021 Bearport Publishing Company. All rights reserved. No part of this publication may be reproduced in whole or in part, stored in any retrieval system, or transmitted in any form or by any means, electronic, mechanical, photocopying, recording, or otherwise, without written permission from the publisher.

For more information, write to Bearport Publishing, 5357 Penn Avenue South, Minneapolis, MN 55419.

Printed in the United States of America.

Contents

Winner! 4
Alexandria's Life 6

Did You Know? 22
Glossary 23
Index 24
Read More 24
Learn More Online 24
About the Author 24

Winner!

Alexandria Ocasio-Cortez couldn't believe it.

She had won her first **election**.

People had voted for her.

Alexandria's Life

Alexandria was born in New York.

Her father was born there, too.

Her mother is from Puerto Rico.

Alexandria with her mother

Alexandria studied hard.

In high school, she loved science.

She even won second place at a science fair.

During college, Alexandria got her start in government.

She wanted to help people have better lives.

She worked for a senator.

Alexandria went to college here.

After college, she worked to help others with school.

Then, Alexandria wanted to be in government.

She wanted to make laws.

In November 2018, Alexandria got her wish.

She was voted into **Congress**.

She was only 29 years old.

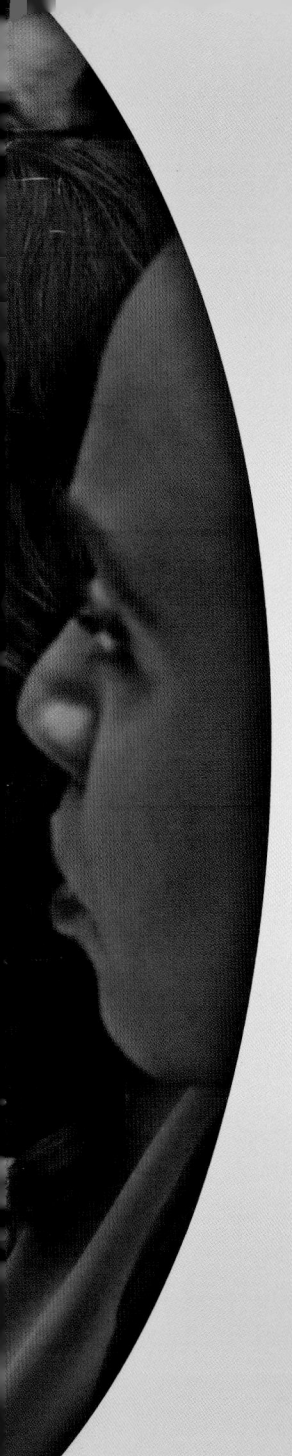

Alexandria has big ideas.

She wants health care for everyone.

She cares about schools and learning.

Alexandria wants to help **immigrants**.

Alexandria also cares about **climate change**.

Earth is getting warmer.

She is trying to fix this big problem.

Alexandria works hard to make new laws.

She is smart, and she is brave.

She wants what is best for all people.

Did You Know?

Born: October 13, 1989

Family: Blanca (mother), Sergio (father), Gabriel (brother)

When she was a kid: She had an **asteroid** named after her. It is called 23238 Ocasio-Cortez!

Special fact: Growing up, her friends called her Sandy. Now, many people call her AOC.

Alexandria says: "No person in America should be too poor to live."

Life Connections

It is important to Alexandria to be brave. She works hard for what she believes in. What do you believe in? How do you make it happen?

Glossary

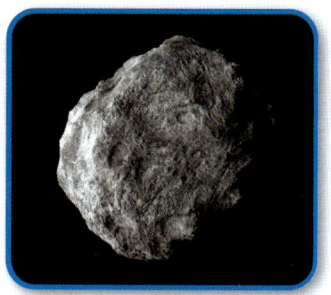

asteroid a rock found in space

climate change changes to weather in a place over time

Congress a part of the U.S. government that makes laws

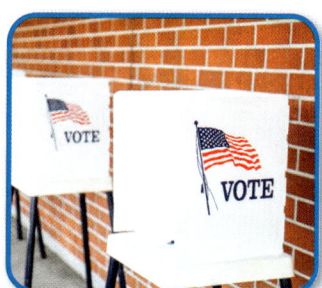

election the act of picking a person for a job

immigrants people who come to live in another country

Index

Congress 14
election 4
government 10, 13
immigrants 17
New York 6
Puerto Rico 6
science 8–9

Read More

Bonwill, Ann. *We Have a Government (Rookie Read-About Civics).* New York: Children's Press (2019).

Boothroyd, Jennifer. *What Are the Branches of Government? (First Step Nonfiction Exploring Government).* Minneapolis: Lerner Publications (2016).

Learn More Online

1. Go to **www.factsurfer.com**
2. Enter "**Alexandria Ocasio-Cortez**" into the search box.
3. Click on the cover of this book to see a list of websites.

About the Author

Rachel Rose was born in Ireland. After she came to live in the United States, she became a citizen. This means she can vote in U.S. elections.